NOV - - 2019

MIDLOTHIAN PUBLIC LIBRARY

3 1614 00199 8112

P9-BZQ-865

CHA

# Tiny Feet
# Between the Mountains

Written and illustrated by

## Hanna Cha

MIDLOTHIAN PUBLIC LIBRARY
14701 S. KENTON AVENUE
MIDLOTHIAN, IL 60445

Simon & Schuster Books for Young Readers

New York London Toronto Sydney New Delhi

O nce upon a time, in a large village between two tall mountains, there was a small child.

Her name was Soe-In, which means "tiny person." When others took two steps, she needed to take four. One handful for others meant three armfuls for Soe-In.

But this never stopped her.

The people in Soe-In's village often competed to see who was the strongest and loudest. They even boasted that they were bigger and more fearless than the spirit tiger rumored to protect the surrounding mountains and forest.

Soe-In would study the
other villagers and complete
each task in her own way.

"How can someone so tiny keep up?" the villagers would whisper to each other. But still, Soe-In refused to give up.

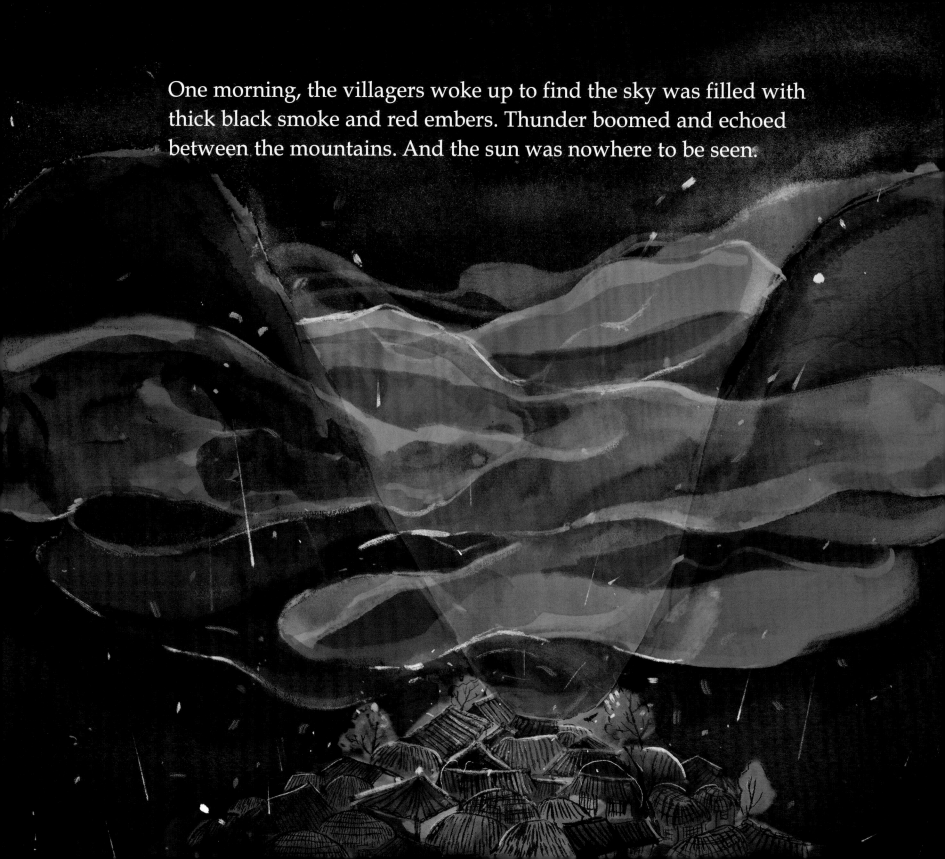

One morning, the villagers woke up to find the sky was filled with thick black smoke and red embers. Thunder boomed and echoed between the mountains. And the sun was nowhere to be seen.

The chieftain asked for a volunteer to go into the mountains and see what had made the sun disappear.

The crowd was silent. When still no one spoke up, Soe-In took a deep breath and said, "Sir, I will go."

Suddenly the villagers' voices rang out.
"You can't even carry my pot! How can
you bring back the sun?"
"You will be lost in those woods!"

Soe-In was startled by the outbursts, but then she
calmly folded up her sleeves and tightened her braid.

The brave little girl knew she had to try.
She ran home to pack her pink bojagi
full of supplies for her journey.

Soe-In knew she was close when she reached the part of the forest where the smoke was the thickest, the hissing sparks were the hottest, and the thunder was the loudest. Suddenly Soe-In stopped dead in her tracks. She couldn't believe her eyes. It was . . .

the spirit tiger!

Soe-In took a step back. She had only ever heard stories about the great spirit tiger. She noticed that heavy tears dripped, dripped, dripped from the tiger's eyes, and his fur was covered in crackling flames.

Looking up, she dared to ask, "Great spirit tiger, what is the matter?"

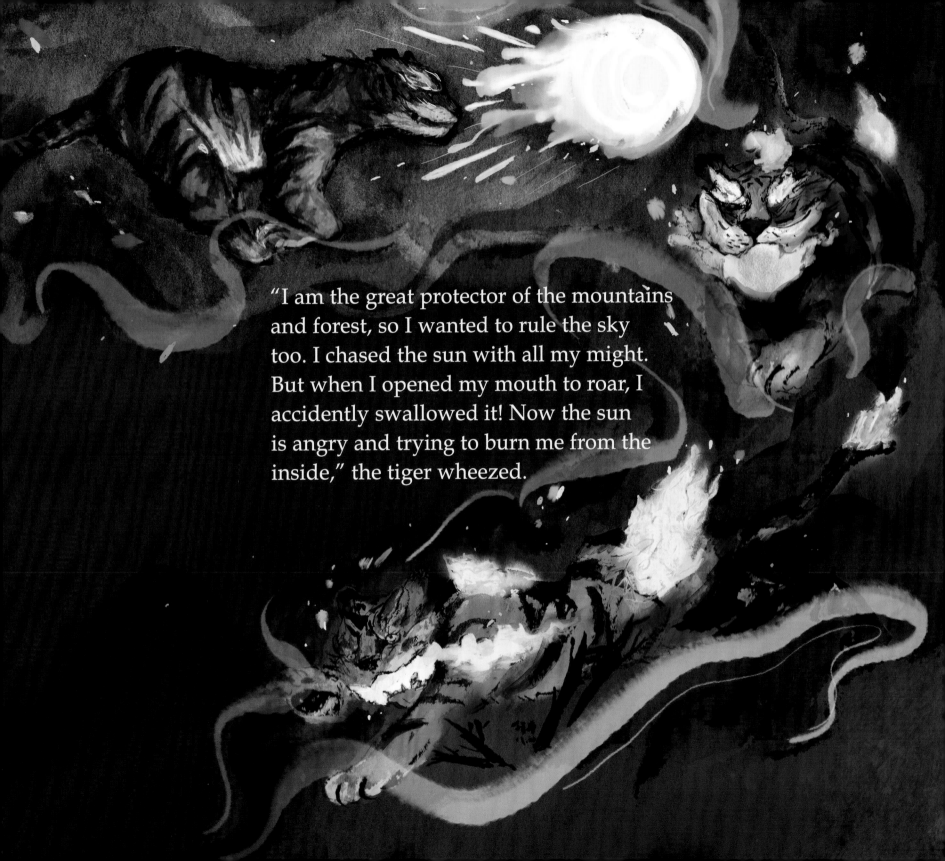

"I am the great protector of the mountains and forest, so I wanted to rule the sky too. I chased the sun with all my might. But when I opened my mouth to roar, I accidently swallowed it! Now the sun is angry and trying to burn me from the inside," the tiger wheezed.

"Let me help you,"
Soe-In said.

He pulled away. "You are a mere tiny child. What can you do?"

The tiger sounded as doubtful as the villagers, but surely, he was wrong about her. "I *can* help," she said. Soe-In took out the bottles from her bojagi. She sprinkled the water on his fur, but there were too many flames to put out.

Remembering the river, she guided the tiger there. But when they got close, the flames on his fur dried up the water. Soe-In tried blanketing the fire with mud instead. But it was no use.

"Maybe the villagers and the spirit tiger are right. Maybe there is nothing that I can do." Soe-In sighed sadly. "I cannot keep up with the flames on the outside."

But then Soe-In got an idea. She'd been so focused on what was happening on the outside that she'd forgotten the real problem was on the *inside*.

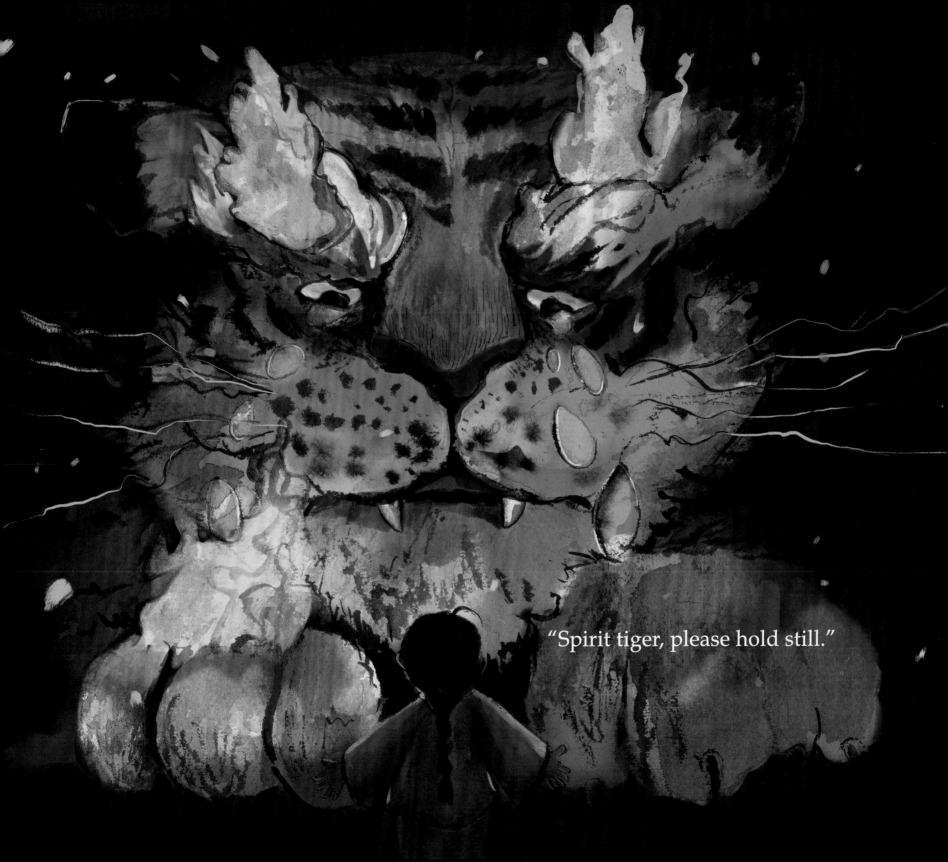

"Spirit tiger, please hold still."

Using her pink bojagi to protect her hands from the flames, Soe-In climbed up the tiger's tail and onto his back. She crawled through the angry, riled fur, using her tiny hands and feet to tickle the tiger.

The spirit tiger began to shake with laughter
until smoke filled his nose and . . .

CHOOOOO!

Losing her footing, Soe-In began to

fall,

fall,

fall….

But the tiger caught her small body in his large paw, his eyes twinkling like stars. He roared with delight.

"I can't believe it! You did it! Thank you for your help!"

"Come! Let me bring you home."

Down in the village, Soe-In could see the people scrambling and yelling with fear at the sight of the spirit tiger. They suddenly looked very tiny.

Soe-In climbed off the tiger and
beckoned the villagers forward.

One by one, they came out and
listened to Soe-In's tale.

When she was finished, Soe-In introduced the villagers
to the spirit tiger. Celebration and cheering erupted as
the spirit tiger kissed Soe-In on the head. He bestowed
a blessing on her and the village before returning to the
mountains and forest.

From that day forward, the villagers were kinder toward Soe-In and she was known as the greatest of them all.

# Author's Note

Long ago in Korea, tigers used to roam freely between the mountains and villages. People would fear the tigers, but at the same time, they saw tigers as a symbol of respect, strength, and dignity. Tigers constantly appeared in Korean stories and images, sometimes as deities, sometimes as threats. Regardless of their role, tigers always offered a moral and guided the Korean people. Many Koreans believed that their country was shaped like a tiger, and that their spirit animals were tigers. Because of colonization, tigers are now extinct in Korea, but their spirit lives on in the strength of the Korean people.

*For my Umma, Appa, and little brother,*
*who taught me love that shines brighter than the sun*

*And to those whom I love so dearly,*
*especially my grand papas*

SIMON & SCHUSTER BOOKS FOR YOUNG READERS

An imprint of Simon & Schuster Children's Publishing Division • 1230 Avenue of the Americas, New York, New York 10020

Copyright © 2019 by Hanna Cha • All rights reserved, including the right of reproduction in whole or in part in any form. SIMON & SCHUSTER BOOKS FOR YOUNG READERS is a trademark of
Simon & Schuster, Inc. • For information about special discounts for bulk purchases, please contact Simon & Schuster Special Sales at 1-866-506-1949 or business@simonandschuster.com.
The Simon & Schuster Speakers Bureau can bring authors to your live event. For more information or to book an event, contact the Simon & Schuster Speakers Bureau at 1-866-248-3049 or visit our website
at www.simonspeakers.com. • Book design by Krista Vossen • The text for this book was set in Book Antiqua • The illustrations for this book were rendered in pen and ink, watercolor, and digitally.
Manufactured in China • 0819 SCP • First Edition • 10 9 8 7 6 5 4 3 2 1 • Library of Congress Cataloging-in-Publication Data • Names: Cha, Hanna, author, illustrator.
Title: Tiny feet between the mountains / Hanna Cha. Description: First edition. | New York : Simon & Schuster Books for Young Readers, [2019] | Summary: In a Korean village where being strong and loud is
valued, tiny Soe-In is ridiculed but when the sun disappears, Soe-In dares to find the spirit tiger and set things right. Includes note about the position of tigers in Korean culture.
Identifiers: LCCN 2018030145 | ISBN 9781534429925 (hardcover : alk. paper) | ISBN 9781534429932 (ebook) | Subjects: | CYAC: Size—Fiction. | Ability—Fiction. | Tigers—Fiction. | Korea—Fiction.
Classification: LCC PZ7.1.C4677 Tin 2019 | DDC [E]—dc23 • LC record available at https://lccn.loc.gov/2018030145